Blue Sky STUDIOS

# THE PEANUTS MOVIE
by SCHULZ

## You've Got Talent, Charlie Brown

based on the *Peanuts* comic strip

by Charles M. Schulz

adapted by Tina Gallo

Ready-to-Read

Simon Spotlight

New York   London   Toronto   Sydney   New Delhi

SIMON SPOTLIGHT
An imprint of Simon & Schuster Children's Publishing Division
1230 Avenue of the Americas, New York, New York 10020
This Simon Spotlight edition September 2015

For information about special discounts for bulk purchases, please contact Simon & Schuster Special Sales at
1-866-506-1949 or business@simonandschuster.com.
Manufactured in the United States of America 0915 LAK
2 4 6 8 10 9 7 5 3
ISBN 978-1-4814-4126-1 (hc)
ISBN 978-1-4814-4125-4 (pbk)
ISBN 978-1-4814-4127-8 (eBook)

This is Charlie Brown.
A little red-haired girl just
moved in across the street
from his house.
He really wants to be her friend,
but he is too nervous to say hi!

Charlie Brown needs advice,
so he visits his pal Lucy.
She loves giving advice!
"I like the Little Red-Haired Girl,"
Charlie Brown tells her.
"How can I become her friend?"

"That's easy," Lucy says.
"Girls like winners. You just need
to become a winner at something."
Charlie Brown decides to follow
Lucy's advice.
He tries to think of something
he does well!

THE DOCTOR

Meanwhile, back at home, Sally decides to enter the school talent show.
"I'm going to be a rodeo star!" she shouts as she jumps onto Snoopy's back.

Charlie Brown decides he will
enter the talent show too.
If he wins the talent show,
maybe the Little Red-Haired Girl
will be his friend!

For days Charlie Brown
works hard on his act.

Soon it is the night of the talent show!
Schroeder starts off the show by playing the piano.
He is a huge hit!

Charlie Brown is backstage,
practicing his magic tricks.
"Abracadabra!" he says,
pulling Snoopy out of a hat!
Then it is time for the rodeo act.
Sally goes onstage.
Charlie Brown hears the audience
laughing at Sally.

It's Charlie Brown to the rescue!
He runs onstage and lets Sally
rope him.
Everyone laughs at him instead of
at Sally! She is a rodeo star!

The next day at school, all the kids point at Charlie Brown and laugh at how silly he was in the show! He's so embarrassed.

"Good grief," he says to himself. He's still happy he helped Sally, but wishes he was also a winner!

After school Charlie Brown
tells Snoopy about his awful day.
"I don't think I'll ever be
a winner," he says.
Snoopy gives him a hug.
At least Snoopy is always there
for him!

Later that evening
Charlie Brown and Snoopy
notice the Little Red-Haired Girl
across the street.
She is dancing!

Charlie Brown remembers there is a dance contest coming up at school.
He wants to learn to dance too.
If they have something in common, maybe the Little Red-Haired Girl will be his friend!

Luckily for Charlie Brown,
Snoopy is a great dancer!
He strikes a tango pose.
He can't wait to teach
Charlie Brown to dance.

Snoopy shows Charlie Brown
how to do his favorite dance steps.
Charlie Brown is a good student
and learns quickly!
"Thanks, Snoopy!" he says.

Charlie Brown is having fun,
so he keeps practicing!
Soon he's able to do everything
Snoopy taught him.
He thinks his dancing will impress
the Little Red-Haired Girl!
Either way, he loves dancing!

Finally it's the night of the dance, and everyone is having a ball! All the kids at school have fun dance steps of their own.

When the dance contest begins, Snoopy puts on sunglasses and becomes Joe Cool!
He shows off his smoothest moves!

Marcie and Peppermint Patty love to dance and it shows! They think they can win, but the contest is not over yet!

Sally pulls Linus onto the
dance floor!
"Come here, my sweet babboo!"
Sally says.
Linus gulps.

It's finally Charlie Brown's
turn to dance.
He performs the dance steps
Snoopy taught him.
Then he makes up his own.
Everyone loves his kooky dance!

His classmates cheer for him!
"That's awesome!" one hollers.
"Go, Charlie Brown!" Linus shouts.
Charlie Brown hopes the
Little Red-Haired Girl is watching!

As he finishes his dance, Charlie Brown kicks off a shoe by mistake and it hits the sprinklers.
Everyone rushes out.
"This isn't how it was supposed to end," Charlie Brown says, putting his shoe back on.
"I thought I had talent.
Now the Little Red-Haired Girl will never be my friend."

The next day at lunch, Linus sees things differently.

"That Little Red-Haired Girl would be lucky to be your friend," he says. "Winner or not, you're a great dancer, brother, and friend!"

Charlie Brown smiles and says, "Maybe I have talent after all!"